Arthur Starter Book 06

ARTHUR
to the Rescue

KB032647

by Marc Brown

Long tail Books

MR. B.

Arthur woke up early with a big smile on his face. He had a whole day to play.

He quickly washed up and got dressed and did all his chores. He didn't want to waste one minute.

D.W.

He started calling his friends to see who was around.
"Sorry," said Buster, "I have to clean my room."

“I can’t come over,” said the Brain.
“I have to help my mom at the shop.”

"I wish I could," said Francine, "but I have to wash the car."

"I'm being held prisoner," Binky whispered. "I have to weed the garden."

Arthur sighed. "Nobody's around," he told his mother.
"What should I do?"
"Well," she said, "you'll just have to play with your imagination."

239.00
TAX CODES

Arthur wasn't sure that would work.

He started thinking . . .

"Whoa!" said Buster. "There was some kind of landslide when I opened the closet."

"Hold on," said Arthur. "I'll have you out in a minute."

TUCKER

"The freezer's not working!" yelled the Brain.
"I've tried everything I can think of to fix it."
"Hold on!" said Arthur. He took a closer look.

“It’s the plug,” said Arthur. He put it back in the socket.

“Thanks, Arthur,” said the Brain. “Another minute and all this ice cream would have melted. We would have been serving ice cream soup!”

"Yikes!" Francine shouted. "The hose is out of control!"
"I'll take care of it," said Arthur.

"Don't worry, Binky. I'll have you out soon."

"Thanks, Arthur. I thought I was doomed for sure."

"What's that noise?" asked Dad.
"Oh, that's just Arthur playing," said Mom.
"It's too bad Arthur's friends were all busy today," said Dad.
"Actually," said Mom, "things worked out fine . . ."